The Tale of the Unicorn

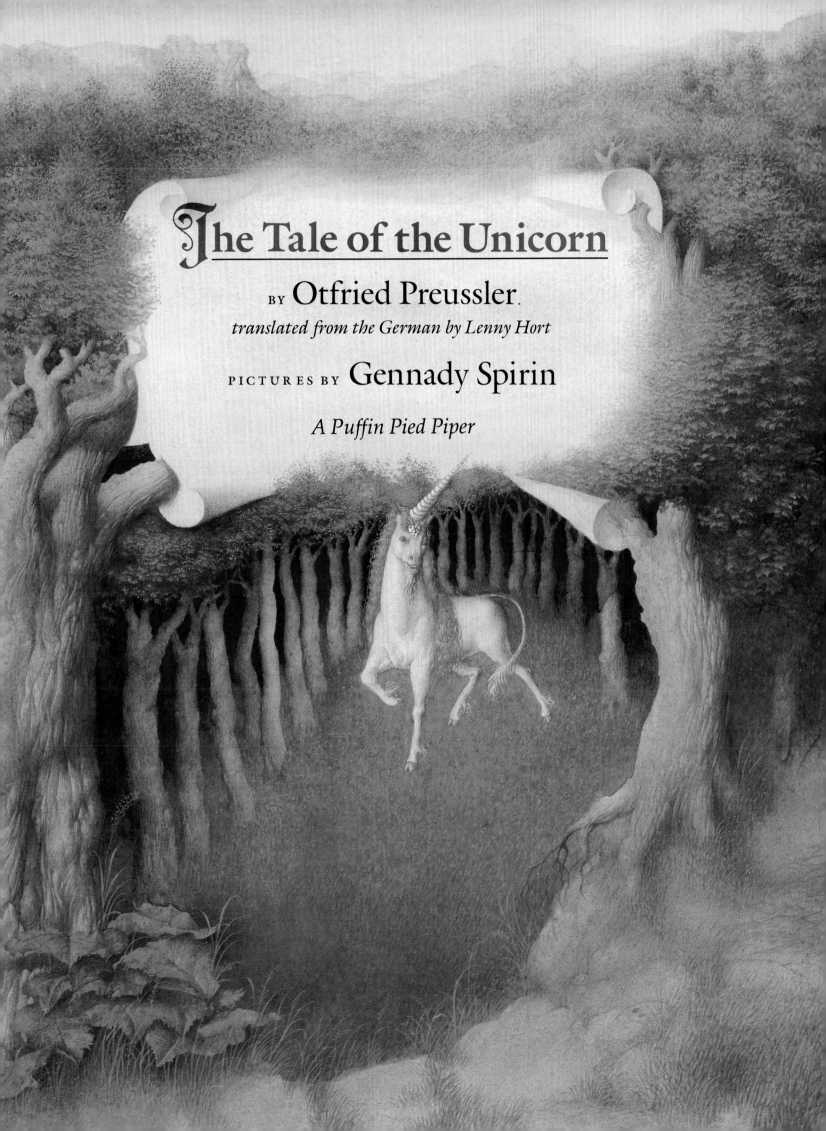

The Tale of the Unicorn

BY Otfried Preussler.

translated from the German by Lenny Hort

PICTURES BY Gennady Spirin

A Puffin Pied Piper

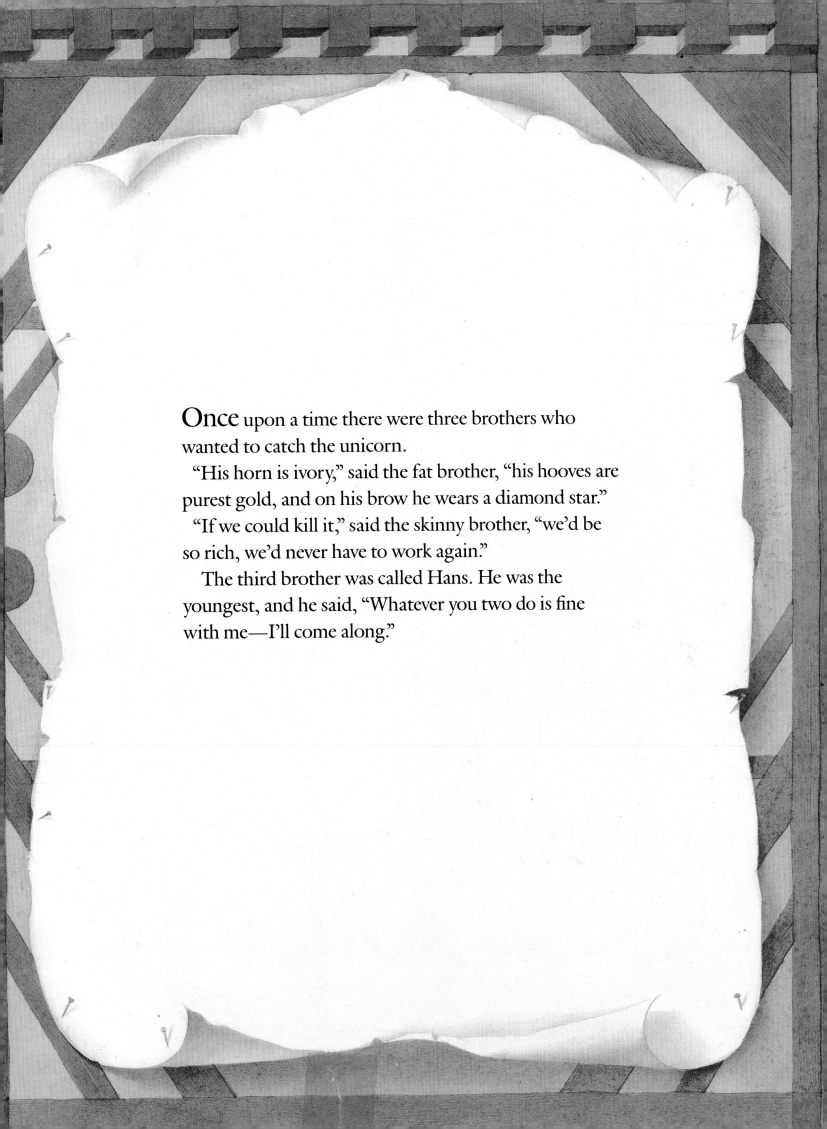

Once upon a time there were three brothers who wanted to catch the unicorn.

"His horn is ivory," said the fat brother, "his hooves are purest gold, and on his brow he wears a diamond star."

"If we could kill it," said the skinny brother, "we'd be so rich, we'd never have to work again."

The third brother was called Hans. He was the youngest, and he said, "Whatever you two do is fine with me—I'll come along."

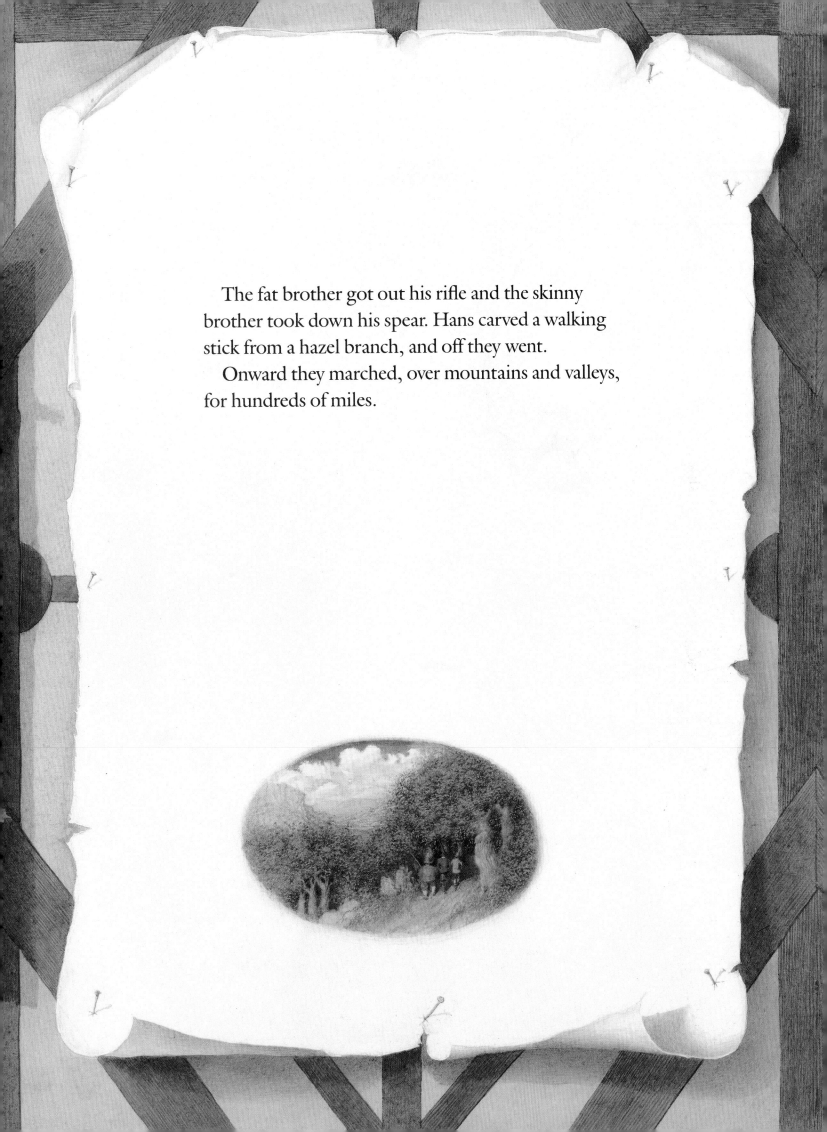

The fat brother got out his rifle and the skinny brother took down his spear. Hans carved a walking stick from a hazel branch, and off they went.

Onward they marched, over mountains and valleys, for hundreds of miles.

After seven-times-seven weeks they came to a village
festival. Outside the inn the peasants all gathered
around a long table, drinking beer and wine, eating
roast goose and suckling pig.

"Won't you come celebrate with us?" the innkeeper
asked the brothers. He introduced them to his plump
and jolly daughter.

As soon as the fat brother learned that she had cooked the entire feast herself, he proposed that they get married at once.

The wedding banquet began on Wednesday and continued from morning to midnight for four whole days. Early Monday morning Hans and the skinny brother set off by themselves to continue the search for the unicorn.

After seven-times-seven weeks they were wandering
through the desert when they found a lump of gold.
"I'm rich!" said the skinny brother. As soon as they
reached a town, he bought a house and fancy clothes.

"I like it here, and here I'll stay!" he called after his brother. "If you still want to catch the unicorn, it's all yours."

Hans slung the rifle over one shoulder and the spear over the other and went on his way.

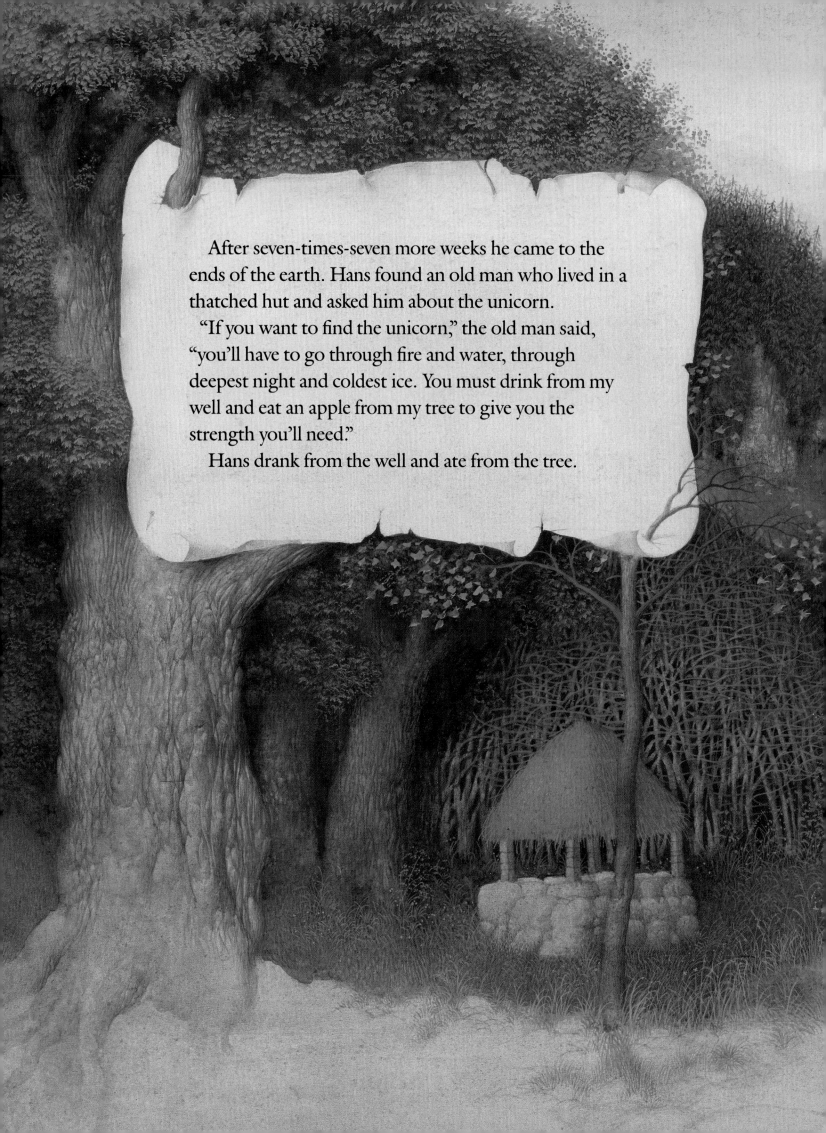

After seven-times-seven more weeks he came to the ends of the earth. Hans found an old man who lived in a thatched hut and asked him about the unicorn.

"If you want to find the unicorn," the old man said, "you'll have to go through fire and water, through deepest night and coldest ice. You must drink from my well and eat an apple from my tree to give you the strength you'll need."

Hans drank from the well and ate from the tree.

Onward he went, through fire and water, through deepest night and coldest ice. One day at last he saw the unicorn grazing quietly in the woods, radiantly beautiful. Its horn was flawless ivory, its hooves were purest gold, and it wore a diamond star on its brow. Slowly Hans raised his rifle. He aimed and felt his finger on the trigger.

Then the unicorn looked over and gazed at him
through its great amber eyes.

"How lovely you are," said Hans.

He dropped the rifle and tossed the spear into the
bushes. And there he stood awestruck, lost to time, lost
to the world.

Eventually he did return home to the world of men and women, his hair now as white as snow. The children all listened in wonder to his story. They knew it was true, that he had gone through fire and water, through deepest night and coldest ice. And when he told them about the unicorn, so bright, so beautiful, grazing peacefully in the woods with the diamond shimmering on its brow, everyone rejoiced that Hans had not pulled the trigger.

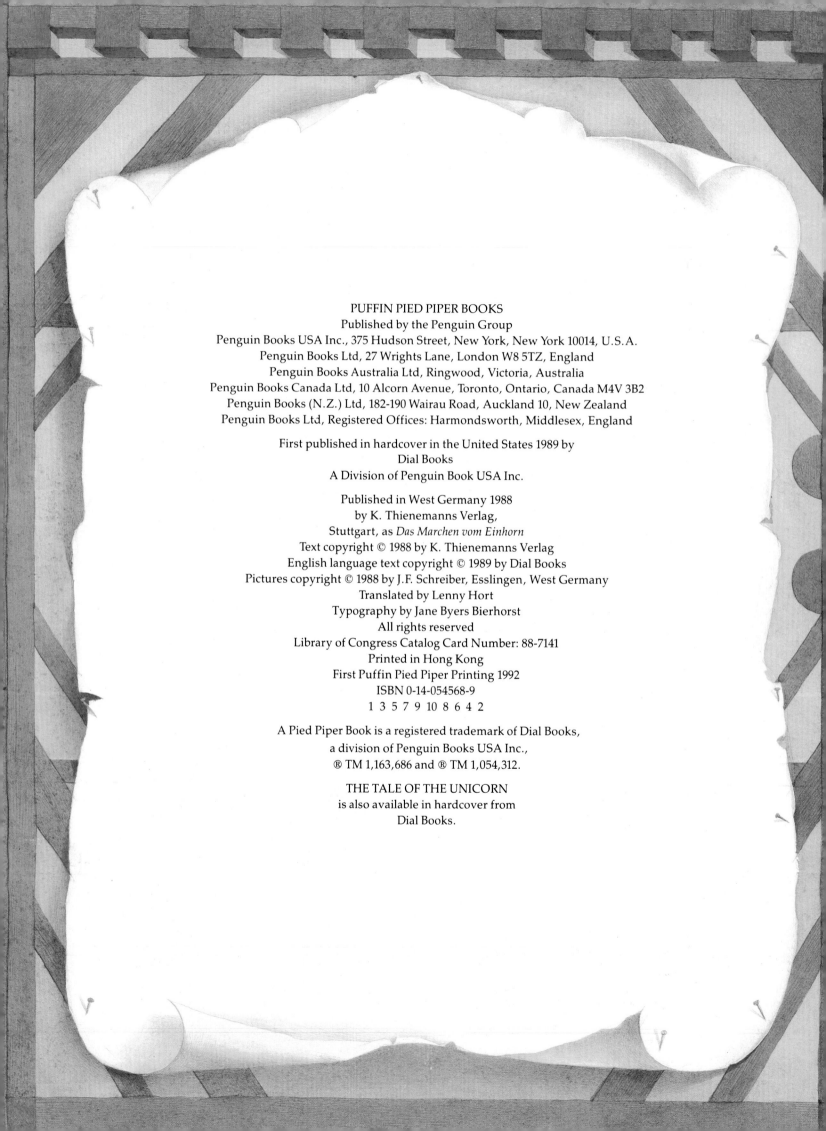

PUFFIN PIED PIPER BOOKS
Published by the Penguin Group
Penguin Books USA Inc., 375 Hudson Street, New York, New York 10014, U.S.A.
Penguin Books Ltd, 27 Wrights Lane, London W8 5TZ, England
Penguin Books Australia Ltd, Ringwood, Victoria, Australia
Penguin Books Canada Ltd, 10 Alcorn Avenue, Toronto, Ontario, Canada M4V 3B2
Penguin Books (N.Z.) Ltd, 182-190 Wairau Road, Auckland 10, New Zealand
Penguin Books Ltd, Registered Offices: Harmondsworth, Middlesex, England

First published in hardcover in the United States 1989 by
Dial Books
A Division of Penguin Book USA Inc.

Published in West Germany 1988
by K. Thienemanns Verlag,
Stuttgart, as *Das Marchen vom Einhorn*
Text copyright © 1988 by K. Thienemanns Verlag
English language text copyright © 1989 by Dial Books
Pictures copyright © 1988 by J.F. Schreiber, Esslingen, West Germany
Translated by Lenny Hort
Typography by Jane Byers Bierhorst
All rights reserved
Library of Congress Catalog Card Number: 88-7141
Printed in Hong Kong
First Puffin Pied Piper Printing 1992
ISBN 0-14-054568-9
1 3 5 7 9 10 8 6 4 2

A Pied Piper Book is a registered trademark of Dial Books,
a division of Penguin Books USA Inc.,
® TM 1,163,686 and ® TM 1,054,312.

THE TALE OF THE UNICORN
is also available in hardcover from
Dial Books.

Otfried Preussler

is widely respected as a children's author not only in his native West Germany but around the world, where his books have appeared in more than 180 separate translations. Titles of his that have previously appeared in America include *The Satanic Mill,* an ALA Notable Book; *The Little Ghost; The Little Witch; Thomas Scarecrow;* and *The Adventures of Strong Vanya.* Mr. Preussler has repeatedly received the German Youth Book Award as well as other international prizes.

Gennady Spirin

was awarded the prestigious Golden Apple at the 1983 Biennale of Illustrations Bratislava. His first book to appear in the United States was *Once There Was a Tree* (Dial) by Natalia Romanova, a *New York Times* Notable Book. *The Boston Globe* described *Once There Was a Tree* as "a magnificent edition that truly represents the child's picture book as an object of art." Also for Dial, Gennady Spirin illustrated *The Enchanter's Spell: Five Famous Tales,* which *Publishers Weekly* called "a glittering collection, timeless and beautiful"; George Sand's *The Mysterious Tale of Gentle Jack and Lord Bumblebee;* and *Boots and the Glass Mountain* by Claire Martin. Mr. Spirin lives in New Jersey with his family.